Dracula Doesn't Play Kickball

Want more Bailey School Kids?

Check these out!

The *Adventures* of
THE BAILEY SCHOOL KIDS #1-48

SUPER SPECIALS #1-6

THE BAILEY CITY **MONSTERS** #1-10

And don't miss the . . .

HOLIDAY SPECIALS

Swamp Monsters Don't Chase Wild Turkeys

Aliens Don't Carve Jack-o'-lanterns

Mrs. Claus Doesn't Climb Telephone Poles

Leprechauns Don't Play Fetch

Ogres Don't Hunt Easter Eggs

Dracula Doesn't Play Kickball

by Debbie Dadey
and
Marcia Thornton Jones

illustrated by John Steven Gurney

A
LITTLE APPLE
PAPERBACK

SCHOLASTIC INC.
New York   Toronto   London   Auckland   Sydney
Mexico City   New Delhi   Hong Kong   Buenos Aires

*To the wonderful students and teachers
in McLeansboro, Illinois, and especially
to David and Marsha Sutton
— DD*

*To Laurie Calkhoven, who has something
even better than GO JUICE — she has motivation,
dedication, and talent!
— MTJ*

No part of this publication may be reproduced in whole or in part, or stored
in a retrieval system, or transmitted in any form or by any means,
electronic, mechanical, photocopying, recording, or otherwise, without
written permission of the publisher. For information regarding permission,
write to Scholastic Inc., Attention: Permissions Department, 557 Broadway,
New York, NY 10012.

ISBN 0-439-56000-4

12 11 10 9 8   12 13 14 15 16/0

Printed in the U.S.A.   40

First printing, February 2004

Contents

1

Twisted

"He's back!" Liza squealed.

"Who's back?" Melody asked. The two girls were hanging out under the oak tree with Eddie and Howie. The four friends liked to meet on the playground each morning before school.

Eddie didn't pay any attention to Liza. He swung like a monkey from a low tree branch. A red ball cap was slung backward on his mass of red hair. He pounded his chest and bellowed, "I am the king of the Bailey School playground. Hear me roar!"

"Let's hear what Liza has to say," Howie told Eddie, "before you fall out of that tree."

Liza looked like she had seen a ghost. Her eyes were round and her lips

trembled. "I saw Mr. Drake and Mrs. Jeepers at the Sheldon City Mall yesterday," she said. "He smiled at me with his big fangs."

Mr. Drake had been their school guidance counselor before he had left to tour with a rock band called BATs. Something about him had always given the kids the creeps. It probably had something to do with the fact that they had thought he was Dracula, the most famous vampire of them all. Of course, the kids also thought that their third-grade teacher, Mrs. Jeepers, was a vampire.

"BATs must be performing in Sheldon City," Howie suggested. The kids lived in Bailey City, but nearby Sheldon City was much bigger and had a lot more concerts.

Eddie jumped down from the tree. "Cool," he said. "Maybe I can get my grandmother to take us over there. Their music is awesome."

"We could," Liza said softly, "if they

were playing, but they're not. The BATs broke up."

Melody nodded. "That happens all the time. Band members play together for a while until they can't get along." Melody's dad had told her all about the rock bands he had listened to when he was a teenager. Only a few of them were still playing songs together.

"If I had a band, it would never break up because I wouldn't let them," Eddie bragged. "I'd be the leader and they'd have to do what I said." Eddie pretended to play an imaginary guitar. He did such a crazy dance his ball cap flew off his head.

"If you had a band," Melody told Eddie, "they would be called the Crazy Trouble-makers."

"Your band would be called the Ding-a-ling-a-lings," Eddie teased Melody.

Howie shook his head. "You should both be in a band together and call it the Twisted Friends."

"Hey," Eddie said with an evil smile,

"that's perfect." Eddie danced around the tree and made up a song. "Twisted. We're so twisted."

Melody couldn't help joining in. She pretended to play the drums while Eddie strummed an air guitar and danced. Melody sang, "Twisted. Twisted. We're twisted friends. We'll stay together until . . ."

". . . the end," Howie sang.

"Yeah," Eddie grunted. "We're twisted."

"I don't know what happened to the BATs," Liza said, ignoring her singing friends. "But I do know what Mr. Drake is going to do next and you're not going to believe it!"

2

Mr. Drake

"What's Mr. Drake going to do?" Melody asked Liza.

"I bet Mr. Drake is going to open up a used car dealership," Howie said. "My mom said we could use a good one in this town."

Eddie snorted. "If Mr. Drake sold cars, they'd be batmobiles."

Melody laughed. "That's a good one, Eddie. But I bet Mr. Drake is coming back to Bailey City to open up a lemonade stand. Remember how he always used to drink pink lemonade? It was like he couldn't live without it."

Eddie held his arms out in front of him and headed straight for Liza's throat. "I am a confused vampire. I must have lemonade. I need sugar. I need lemons."

7

Liza pushed Eddie away. "It's worse than any of that," she told them. "Mr. Drake is coming back to work at our school."

"Why would anyone come to Bailey School unless they had to?" Eddie said seriously.

"There's only one reason why Mr. Drake would come back here," Liza said. "He's the one and only Count Dracula. He must have found a cure for the allergies that drove him away from Bailey School in the first place."

"You're as nutty as peanut butter," Eddie told her.

"It all makes sense," Liza argued. "He's hungry and he needs fresh blood."

"Oh, my gosh!" Melody squealed. "You might be right. Bailey City is like a vampire hideout. We're the only ones who suspect there are vampires around."

A few months ago, Mr. Drake had been the school's counselor and the kids had been sure he had turned Huey and Ben into little vampires. It had turned out they had just had colds, but that didn't mean Mr. Drake wasn't a vampire.

"Mr. Drake must have come back for a vampire recharge," Liza said.

"Is he going to be our guidance counselor again?" Howie asked. He shuddered at the idea. After all, Mr. Drake's office had looked like a dark, creepy bat cave.

Liza shook her head. "Principal Davis already hired Miss Lagoon to be the new counselor. The only job Mr. Drake could find was being playground monitor. It doesn't pay as much, but Mr. Drake says he thinks he'll like it. Besides, I heard him tell Mrs. Jeepers he has another job lined up."

"There he is," Eddie told Melody. "You can ask him yourself."

The four kids watched a dark figure dart in and out of the shadows. Mr. Drake was dressed entirely in black — he even wore black cowboy boots. The collar on his black jacket was pulled up so it nearly

covered his cheeks. On his head was a black ball cap that cast a dark shadow over his face. He carried a black leather duffel bag and a bottle filled with a thick, red liquid. Next to all the black, Mr. Drake's skin looked as pale as brittle bones. He flashed his fangs at the kids and then took a swig from the bottle. Red liquid dribbled from his fangs.

"I thought he only drank lemonade," Liza said with a shaky voice.

"That was the old Mr. Drake," Eddie said. "Maybe the new Mr. Drake likes to drink something else."

"Yeah," Melody said, "like fresh blood."

3

No Ordinary Juice

Eddie didn't think the morning would ever end. "Work, work, work," he mumbled. "That's all we ever do."

"Shh," Melody warned. She glanced at the front of the room to make sure their teacher wasn't looking.

Melody and her friends thought Mrs. Jeepers was a vampire. After all, she lived in a haunted house and kept a long wooden coffinlike box in her basement. She even came from Transylvania — just like Mr. Drake.

"We have to work," Howie whispered, "or Mrs. Jeepers will get mad."

Eddie sighed. "Having a vampire for a teacher sure makes it hard to have any fun," he huffed. "I can't wait for recess."

Liza's face turned as pale as the pages in her notebook. "How can we have fun with Count Dracula as our playground monitor?" she whimpered.

"No one is going to stop me from having fun," Eddie said. "Recess is my favorite part of the day."

When it was finally time for recess, Eddie pushed aside a girl named Carey and jumped in front of his classmate Huey to be first in line. "Hurry," Eddie said to Howie, Melody, and Liza.

Liza didn't hurry. She slowly pulled herself up from her desk and walked toward the line.

"If you don't speed up, you'll be the last one outside," Eddie told her. Liza shrugged, but she didn't go any faster.

When Mrs. Jeepers led them out into the hall, she bumped into Mr. Drake. He stood in the doorway of the classroom next door, talking to Mr. Tate.

"This stuff makes all the difference in

the world," Mr. Drake was saying to the fourth-grade teacher. Mr. Drake's voice was hoarse and he spoke with the same strange accent as Mrs. Jeepers. He held out a bottle filled with a deep red liquid, just like the one the kids had seen earlier.

Mrs. Jeepers smiled an odd little half smile and gave a tiny nod. "Mr. Drake speaks the truth," she told Mr. Tate. "I have tried his special blend myself."

Mr. Tate took the bottle from Mr. Drake and looked closely at the label. The fourth-grade teacher's eyes were bloodshot and underlined by heavy bags. "Maybe I do need to try this," Mr. Tate said. "Thanks." He opened the bottle and took a big swig of the thick, red liquid.

Liza gasped before pulling Melody and Howie out of the line and down a side hall. Eddie paused to look at the rest of the kids heading toward the playground door. Then he sighed and hurried in the

other direction after Liza and his other two friends.

"Did you see that?" Liza asked.

Melody and Howie nodded, but Eddie put his hands on his hips. "What I saw was the rest of our class and the entire fourth grade beating us outside," he said. "Now, what's your problem?"

Liza drew a shaky breath before continuing. "Mr. Drake is giving other teachers some of his specially blended drink."

"So?" Eddie huffed. "Teachers drink coffee all the time. Now they're drinking juice. What's the big deal?"

"That's no ordinary juice and you know it," Melody said.

Liza whimpered. "It's bottled blood made just for vampires," she said. "And there is only one reason why Mr. Tate would be drinking blood. Mr. Drake has already turned him into a vampire!"

"We don't know that for sure," Howie pointed out. "We don't even know for a fact that Mr. Drake is Count Dracula. Let's think this through."

"I don't have time to think," Eddie sputtered. "I only have time for recess."

"Eddie has a point," Howie said. "If we're caught lurking in the hallways instead of playing outside, we could get in trouble."

"Now you're talking," Eddie said. Eddie led the way down the hall, but the closer they came to the playground door, the slower Liza walked. "Come on," Eddie said to Liza. "Why are you going so slow? Are you sick or something?"

"That's it," Liza said. "I must be sick. I'd better go to the nurse's office."

"What's with her?" Eddie asked as they watched Liza hurry down the hall in the opposite direction.

Melody shrugged. "I think she's afraid of seeing Mr. Drake at recess."

"Who cares about Mr. Drake?" Eddie said. "He won't be able to catch me. I'm

faster than a speeding bullet." To prove it, Eddie zipped out the door onto the playground.

Melody looked at Howie. "I just hope Eddie is faster than a swooping vampire bat."

4

Captain Eddie

Mr. Drake stood under the oak tree. He was wearing sunglasses, a black ball cap, and a long-sleeved T-shirt. He was just finishing rubbing sunscreen on his nose and forehead when the kids saw him. Mr. Drake smiled, revealing his pointy eye-teeth. When he stepped out from the shadows, he held a huge black umbrella over his head to protect his skin from the sun.

Kids ran helter-skelter on the playground. Eddie knocked a ball away from some girls playing dodgeball. Then he pushed aside two kids who were heading for the swings.

Suddenly, a sharp piercing sound brought all the kids to a dead stop. Even Eddie turned around to see where the noise had come from.

"Gather round," Mr. Drake called to the kids after blowing a huge black whistle one more time.

"What's this all about?" Eddie mumbled.

"I bet he's going to tell us about playground rules," Howie said.

"Rules are for fools," Eddie griped. "He's wasting my valuable playground time."

All the third and fourth graders hurried to cluster around the new playground monitor. The kids had to listen extra hard to hear Mr. Drake's low, hoarse voice.

"Today," he said, "we will all play an organized game of kickball. Now, let us divide into two teams."

"Kickball?" Eddie said. "Organized? I don't want to play anything organized."

Mr. Drake looked at Eddie and licked his lips. "I remember you from when I was a counselor here," he said. "Perhaps you could be the captain of one of the teams?"

"Captain?" Eddie said with a grin. "That doesn't sound so bad. We'll have the best team ever with me in charge," he bragged.

Mr. Drake chose a fourth grader as captain of the other team. Unfortunately, he chose Ben. Ben was known as the biggest bully in Bailey School and Eddie didn't like the fact that Ben got more attention.

Eddie stepped in front of Ben. "I'll pick first," Eddie said.

Melody and Howie got ready to move to Eddie's team, but Eddie didn't pick them first. He didn't pick them second, either. In fact, Eddie didn't pick them until the very end. He picked the biggest fourth graders instead. "Sorry about that," Eddie told Melody and Howie. "But I have to have the fastest and strongest players so I can beat the pants off Ben's team."

Melody stuck out her chin, but Howie nodded. He knew he wasn't the best kickball player on the playground. Melody was about to tell Eddie a thing or two about who was better at what, but Eddie didn't give her a chance.

"I'm up first," Eddie yelled as he pushed his way to the front of the line so he could be the first to kick.

Ben grinned at Eddie and then rolled the ball so fast it looked like a blur. Eddie got ready to kick, but he missed and the ball ended up rolling off the field.

"Strike one," Ben called out, and a few of the kids on his team giggled.

"No, it isn't," Eddie said. "There was dust in my eyes. I get another chance."

Ben rolled the ball and Eddie kicked again. This time the ball rolled out-of-bounds.

"Strike two," Ben yelled. A few more kids snickered.

"You're not rolling it straight," Eddie said to Ben.

"Am, too," Ben said. Then he pitched the ball a third time.

Eddie kicked at the ball for all he was worth. Unfortunately, he kicked too soon. Eddie missed and landed on the seat of his pants. The ball popped up and bounced on his head.

"Strike three!" Ben yelled. "You're out!"

"Am not," Eddie called out, scrambling to his feet. "I call a do-over!"

"No, you don't," somebody on Ben's team said. "You can't have two turns in a row."

While Eddie and the rest of the kids argued, Melody and Howie huddled off to the side.

"It looks like Captain Eddie is the strike-out pro," Melody said with a giggle.

Howie nodded. "I wonder if Mr. Drake will blow his whistle."

They looked at Mr. Drake. He stood in the shadows of the giant oak tree, watching Eddie very closely. Finally, Mr. Drake blew his whistle. "Play ball," he yelled. Eddie slammed the ball out of his way and stomped toward the end of the kicking line.

"What if Mr. Drake really did come

back to suck our blood?" Howie asked Melody.

Eddie was walking by when he heard Howie. "You're dumber than dirt," Eddie said. "You're wasting your recess time with this vampire talk. We have nothing to worry about. After all, I'm positive that Dracula doesn't play kickball."

"How do you know that?" Melody asked. "For all we know, vampires play kickball all the time."

Eddie laughed. "If they did," he said, "they'd call the championship the Dracula World Kickball Cup."

Howie sighed. "If that were true, I know what that cup would be full of," he said. "Blood. Human blood."

"I wonder if vampires get trophies," Eddie wondered out loud.

Howie nodded. "Yeah, the trophies probably have really big teeth on them, too."

Eddie laughed. "I bet dentists love vampires. They probably get charged extra for teeth cleaning."

Melody rolled her eyes. "Will you guys stop joking around?"

Eddie looked at Melody. "Why?" he asked. "I'm in third grade. I'm a boy. It's recess. Give me one good reason why I shouldn't joke around."

Melody's eyes got really big as she looked past Eddie. "There!" she screamed. "There's a really good reason!"

5

King of All Vampires

Howie, Liza, Eddie, and a bunch of Ben's team members raced over to Carey. Mr. Drake was bent over her. Melody expected to see Mr. Drake's fangs covered in blood, but Mr. Drake just pulled Carey up from the ground.

"Thank you," Carey told Mr. Drake. She wiped her hands on her pants before batting her eyelashes at Eddie and smiling. Her eyelashes reminded Eddie of fluttering bat wings.

"I slipped when I tried to catch the ball," she said with a giggle. Carey always seemed to giggle whenever Eddie was around.

Eddie rolled his eyes and stomped back to the sidelines. Melody and Howie stood behind him.

"I think Carey was disappointed you didn't pick her for your team," Howie said.

"Why would I pick Carey?" Eddie asked. "She can't kick. She can't catch. And she's as slow as marshmallow cream."

"But she likes you," Melody pointed out. "I mean, *really* likes you."

Eddie gagged and then an evil smile spread across his face. "Maybe we should tell Mr. Drake to bite Carey," he teased. "If she turned into a vampire, she might fly away for good and I'd never be bothered by her again."

"How can you say that?!" Melody gasped.

"It was just a joke," Eddie said with a shrug.

Huey kicked a ball out to left field. Carey ran hard to catch it, but she wasn't fast enough. Huey made it to first base.

"All right," Eddie cheered. "Now we're getting somewhere. Howie, you're next."

Ben sneered at Howie. "You couldn't kick this ball if I glued it to your toe."

Howie's hands were sweating as the

ball rolled toward him. He watched the ball until it got close and then he blasted it with his foot. The ball flew high over Ben's head and far out onto the playground.

"Go, Howie!" Melody cheered.

"That's my friend," Eddie yelled to the rest of the team.

Melody stopped cheering when she saw Mr. Drake. He stood in the shadows of the school, talking to one of the fifth-grade teachers. Melody couldn't help but notice Mr. Drake pulling out a bottle of red juice

from his duffel bag and handing it to the teacher.

"I'm worried about Mr. Drake and that strange red stuff," Melody whispered to Eddie.

Eddie laughed. "Who cares?" he said. "We're winning! If Luke kicks this ball far enough, we can get three runs."

"How can you think of kickball at a time like this?" Melody asked.

"This is the perfect time to think about kickball," he told her. "In case you haven't noticed, we're in the middle of a kickball game. Besides, Mr. Drake is probably just one of the those weird people who drinks tomato juice or something disgusting like that." Eddie laughed at his own joke.

"This isn't funny. The king of all vampires is invading our playground!" Melody said, putting her hands on her hips. "I am not going to joke around while Mr. Drake turns our whole school into a vampire amusement park. I'm going to do something!"

6

Sick of Vampires

Luckily, Mr. Drake didn't see Melody run toward the school building and slip inside. The building seemed dark to Melody after the bright sunlight on the playground. Melody hoped she wouldn't run into Mrs. Jeepers. The thought of meeting a vampire teacher in a dark hallway gave her the creeps.

Melody's tennis shoes tapped down the hallway. She sighed with relief when she reached the main office. The secretary, Mrs. Lucky, smiled at her. "How can I help you?" Mrs. Lucky asked.

"I . . . I need to see the nurse," Melody said.

"You're not the only one," Mrs. Lucky told her. "There's a terrible flu bug going around. I hope you're not catching it."

"Me, too," Melody said as she slipped inside the nurse's room. An eye chart hung on the wall next to a big scale for weighing kids. Liza was lying on a cot in the corner. The nurse was humming to herself with her back turned to the girls.

"Liza," Melody whispered softly. "I need your help."

Liza shook her head. "No way! I'm sick."

"You're just sick of vampires," Melody said. "You're faking."

"I'm as serious as a broken video game," Liza said. Her voice sounded hoarse and her forehead was wrinkled in a frown.

Melody had to admit that her friend didn't look well, but she wouldn't give up. "We have to think of a way to get rid of Mr. Drake."

"I'm not going anywhere," Liza said. "The nurse was just about to take my temperature."

With that, the nurse turned around and noticed Melody for the first time. "Oh,

35

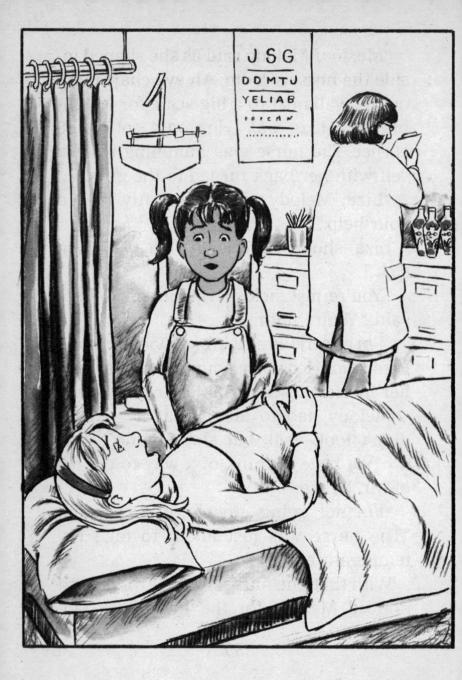

dear," the nurse said, holding up a ther-mometer. "Do I have another patient?"

Melody nodded her head. "Yes," she said. "I mean, no. I mean, I'm feeling much better now." Melody turned to leave but stopped short when she saw three familiar bottles sitting on the counter.

She gasped and the nurse had her sit down beside Liza. Melody felt dizzy, but it wasn't because of a flu bug. There, sitting on the nurse's desk, were three bottles of Mr. Drake's red potion. Beneath the bottles was something even worse. When the nurse wasn't looking, Melody snatched the something worse off the counter and stuffed it in her pocket. She couldn't wait to show her friends.

7

Epidemic

After school, Melody met Eddie, Liza, and Howie under the oak tree. The wind whispered through the leaves as if it were telling secrets.

"I thought you were sick," Howie said to Liza. "Why didn't you go home?"

"I'd go home quicker than you can say 'blood and guts,'" Eddie said. "In fact, I'd go anywhere besides school."

Liza sighed and shook her head. "I didn't have a temperature, so the nurse wouldn't let me call my mom."

"You were faking," Melody said. "I knew it all along."

"Was not," Liza said. Her lip trembled and she looked like she might cry. "My stomach feels like vampire bats are fluttering around inside it."

"You're not the only one with vampire trouble," Melody said.

"I know," Liza told her. "The nurse said lots of kids have been complaining of a bug."

"I'm not talking about sick kids," Melody said. "I'm talking about an epidemic of batty teachers."

Eddie nodded seriously. "That's nothing new," he said. "Teachers have always been batty."

Howie noticed how Melody's voice shook. He ignored Eddie and faced Melody. "What are you trying to tell us, Melody?" Howie asked.

"Mr. Drake is Count Dracula and that means we're all in danger," Melody explained. "Wherever vampires hang around, there's sure to be trouble."

"Not necessarily," Howie said. "Bats can be very helpful. They eat insects."

"I don't think Mr. Drake would be the insect-eating kind of bat," Melody said. "He would be the bite-you-on-the-

neck-and-suck-all-your-blood kind of bat."

"Now, let's think about this logically," Howie said. "We've known Mr. Drake and Mrs. Jeepers for a while and I haven't heard of a single person getting their blood sucked dry."

"It's only a matter of time," Melody said. "Vampires are known to slowly gather in an area. Then they sneak around at night, attacking their victims while they sleep. Lots of people don't even know they've been bitten until it's too late."

"Too late?" Liza squeaked.

Melody nodded. "One. Two. Three bites. And then it happens. The poor helpless victim turns into a vampire monster just like that." She snapped her fingers and Liza jumped.

"You're worrying about nothing," Eddie pointed out. "You don't even know if Mr. Drake really is a vampire."

"You're absolutely right," Melody said.

"I am?" Eddie asked.

"Yep," Melody told them. "We don't have to worry about being vampire bait," she said, "at least not for now."

Liza smiled until Melody finished her thought. "Mr. Drake didn't come back to Bailey City to turn kids into vampires." Melody continued, "He came back to turn all our *teachers* into vampires!"

Howie smiled and Liza shook her head. Eddie laughed out loud. "I think you've gone batty yourself," Eddie told her. "Our teachers may all be monsters, but except for Mrs. Jeepers, they're not the blood-sucking type. They're more like the work-you-until-you're-dead type of monster teachers."

"You won't be so sure when I tell you what I found in the nurse's office," Melody said.

"You snooped?" Liza asked.

Melody nodded.

"I'm proud of you," Eddie told her.

"What did you find?" Howie wanted to know.

Melody looked over her shoulder to make sure no one else was near enough to see. She pulled the paper she had taken from the nurse's office out of her pocket. "It's a notice from Mr. Drake," Melody said. "He's called a teachers' meeting. That can mean only one thing. Mr. Drake already has all the teachers in his evil grasp."

"Ridiculous," said Liza.

"Preposterous," said Howie.

"Baloney," said Eddie.

"Then you'll come with me to the teachers' meeting?" Melody asked.

"To the teachers' meeting?" Eddie said, his voice cracking.

"Yes," Melody said. "We'll meet here tonight, just as the sun goes down."

"Isn't that the best time for vampires to bite?" Liza asked nervously.

"Of course it is," Melody said. "It's also

the best time to find out for ourselves what Mr. Drake is up to."

"I'm not sure this is such a good idea," Howie told his friends.

"Of course it isn't," Eddie said. "It's a stupid, crazy, awful idea."

Melody nodded. "And it's exactly what we're going to do."

8

Vampire Convention

The sun hung low in the sky and shadows stretched across the playground like long, bony skeleton fingers as Melody made her way across the playground. Liza, Howie, and Eddie were already waiting under the oak tree.

"School is scary enough in the daytime," Eddie said. "But it's a nightmare after the sun goes down."

"It's going to get scarier if we don't do something about Count Dracula's teacher takeover," Melody warned them.

"You're jumping to conclusions," Howie said. "We don't know anything for sure."

"We'll know very soon," Melody said, her mouth set in a straight line. "Now, let's get this over with. Follow me."

"I'll be the leader," Eddie said. "Follow me."

Melody put her hands on her hips and stood in front of Eddie. "No! Spying on this meeting was my idea, so I'm the leader."

"You are not," Eddie said, tossing his cap to the ground.

While Melody and Eddie argued, Liza and Howie rolled their eyes. "Let's go," Liza told Howie. "I'm tired and I want to get this over with so I can go home and sleep."

Howie and Liza left their two friends in the shadow of the tree and headed toward the school.

"Hey!" Eddie called. "Where are you going?"

"We came here on a mission," Liza said, "and we're going to get it done."

"You can't do it without me," Eddie said.

"Or me," Melody argued, pushing her way in front of Eddie.

"We won't be able to do it at all if you keep arguing," Howie pointed out.

Melody glared at Eddie. Eddie stuck out his tongue at Melody, but they stopped arguing. The kids crept toward the school and slowly opened the side door. They paused when it squeaked, waiting to see if anyone had heard. The hallways were deathly still.

After taking a deep breath, Liza stepped foot inside the building. Her three friends followed. They sneaked down the dark halls toward a single door that spilled light into the hallway. Very slowly, the four friends peered around the door.

The teachers were there, all right. It looked as though teachers from as far away as Sheldon City had come to the meeting. They all sat in a circle. Mr. Drake stood in the center behind a table that was piled high with bottles. Beside each teacher was a tiny cup full of red juice.

"It's a vampire convention!" Melody
gasped.

Mr. Drake's head snapped up as if he'd
heard a noise. Then he slowly turned and
looked right at the four kids.

They froze in fear.

"Run!" Eddie yelled.

9

Vampire Teachers

"What are we going to do?" Liza asked her friends the next morning before school. She shivered and pulled her sweater tight. The kids were under the big oak tree on the playground, waiting for the bell to ring.

"Just think," Melody said slowly, "a school full of teachers just like Mrs. Jeepers."

"One Mrs. Jeepers is bad enough," Howie said.

"Until we think of what to do, we have to stay out of trouble," Melody said. "The last thing we need to do is make a nest of vampire teachers angry."

Eddie pushed Melody aside. "You don't have proof that Mr. Drake is turning teachers into blood-sucking vampires!"

"What about last night's teacher convention?" Liza asked. "How do you explain that?"

"For all we know, Mr. Drake is trying to get his band, BATs, going again," Eddie said. "So he invited teachers for an audition session."

"A rock-and-roll band of teachers?" Howie gasped. "What kind of music would they play?"

"Funeral marches," Eddie said matter-of-factly. "But my point is, we don't have to do anything Melody says."

"Yes, you do," Melody told him. "I happen to know more about vampires than you do."

Eddie pointed his finger at Melody. "You're not my boss," he said.

"And you're not my friend," Melody said, pushing Eddie's hand away.

Liza stood between her friends. "Come on, guys. Let's not fight at a time like this."

"Liza's right," Howie said. "We need to work together."

Eddie stared at his friends. Then he looked at Melody. "I'm not doing anything with her. I'm tired of her bossing me around. And if you're siding with her, I'm not doing anything with you guys, either."

"You mean, you're breaking up our group?" Liza asked, her lip trembling. "That's what happened to Mr. Drake and the BATs."

Eddie glared at them all and marched away as a cold wind howled through the limbs on the old oak tree.

10

Purple Lips and Bloody Noses

Eddie was determined not to do anything Melody said. In fact, he misbehaved every chance he got. During spelling time, Eddie talked to Huey and ate a snack. Liza held her breath, but Mrs. Jeepers didn't punish him. Instead, she smiled and took a sip from a bottle just like Mr. Drake's. When she dabbed at a red drop on her chin, it stained her white napkin.

In art class, Eddie painted big purple lips on the side of his fist. Then he went around kissing everyone with his fist. In no time at all, every kid in the class had big purple smears on their cheeks. Everyone except Eddie, that is. Howie glanced at their art teacher to see if she'd send Eddie to the principal's office, but she just smiled. Then she took a big sip from one of Mr. Drake's bottles.

"This is great," Eddie said in the hallway on the way back from art class. "I can do anything I want. The teachers don't care as long as they have their juice to drink."

Melody overheard Eddie bragging. "How can he say that?" she whispered to Howie and Liza. "Doesn't he know what's really in those bottles?"

"Maybe we could sneak into the teachers' rooms and swipe all the bottles," Howie suggested.

Liza gasped. "That would be stealing."

Howie nodded. "Yeah, but we'd be doing it to help them."

Melody shook her head. "No, then they'd have to get their blood from somewhere else — like our necks! We have to think of another plan before Eddie does something we'll all regret."

At recess, Eddie ignored Mr. Drake, who watched the kids from the shade.

Eddie grabbed the kickball and insisted on being a kickball captain again.

"I don't care about kickball," Melody whispered to Howie and Liza. "I just want to get rid of all these vampires."

Carey had other ideas. She wanted Eddie to pay attention to her. "Yoo-hoo," she called to Eddie. "Pick me for your team, Eddie. You won't be sorry." She batted her eyes and blew a kiss.

Eddie jumped to the right, pretending to dodge her kiss. When he did, he ran right into Ben.

Ben stumbled out of the way. "Are you going to strike out again today, squirt?" Ben asked.

"You wish," Eddie snapped. "We're going to beat you so badly, you'll be crying for your mama."

Ben laughed. "Wah, wah, I'm shivering in my booties."

Eddie held up his fists like he was ready to fight.

"Cut it out," Howie warned. "Before Mr. Drake swoops over here.

Liza sniffled and pulled a tissue out of her pants pocket. "I think my nose is going to bleed." Liza's nose always bled when she got really scared.

"Let's grab Eddie before he gets a bloody nose, too," Howie said.

"You're right," Melody agreed. "If vampires see bloody noses, it could send them into a feeding frenzy!"

Liza, Howie, and Melody rushed over and pulled Eddie away from Ben. "You have to help us do something about Mr. Drake," Melody told Eddie.

"I don't have to do anything," Eddie snapped.

"You're our friend," Melody said. "And friends stick together."

Eddie shook his head. "I'm not your friend anymore."

"I don't feel well," Liza said, putting her hand on her forehead.

"See what you're doing?" Melody told Eddie. "You're making Liza sick."

"You're *both* upsetting her," Howie pointed out. "Let's calm down and figure out what to do about Mr. Drake."

"I don't have time to go on a wild vampire chase," Eddie said. "I have to beat the pants off Ben's team."

"This isn't a matter of winning or losing," Melody said. "It's a matter of life and death!"

11

Dracula Cure

"Nothing is more important than winning," Eddie said. He turned and started bossing the rest of the team. "My team goes first," he yelled.

"No way," Ben yelled. "You went first last time. And you still lost!"

"That was just a practice game," Eddie told him. "It didn't count."

"Did, too," Ben told him, taking a step closer to Eddie.

"Did not," Eddie said, walking up to Ben.

"Did!" Ben yelled.

"Didn't!" Eddie yelled back. Then Eddie did something stupid. Very stupid. He pushed Ben.

Nobody likes being pushed — especially Ben. Ben shoved Eddie. When Eddie regained his balance, his face was red and his hands were curled into fists. Eddie didn't waste a moment. He went right for Ben, and Ben was ready for him.

"Stop!" Liza yelled.

"Fight!" a kid named Jake yelled.

"Break it up!" a couple of kids called out.

Ben and Eddie didn't hear a word. They were too mad to listen to the kids that encircled them.

Suddenly, a shadow fell over the fighting boys. Mr. Drake pushed his way through the group of kids. He held his umbrella high over his head and licked his lips. But then Mr. Drake accidentally dropped his umbrella and let out a hoarse yell when the sun touched the skin on his face. He reached out and pulled Eddie and Ben apart.

"Enough," Mr. Drake said. "As team captains, it is your responsibility to set a good example. You both have failed."

Eddie sputtered and tried to pull away

from Mr. Drake's clutches. "But . . ." The word died in Eddie's mouth as Mr. Drake's hand tightened on Eddie's shoulder. Mr. Drake leaned close to Eddie.

Tiny beads of sweat had formed on Mr. Drake's pale skin and his lips stretched back over his teeth in a snarl. "Step into the shade and we will discuss this. If that is what you truly desire."

Mr. Drake led Eddie and Ben away and took them into the shadows of the school.

"Oh, no," Liza squealed. "Mr. Drake is going to bite Eddie."

"Good," Melody snapped. "Eddie deserves it! He's been acting rotten. He's been bossy and causing trouble all day. Not only that, he's the one who broke up our group."

Howie shook his head. "Nobody deserves to be turned into a vampire," Howie said. "No matter what they've done."

"We have to help him," Liza said, holding her hand over her stomach. Her lips were set in a grim line and they looked a little green. "This is making me feel very sick."

"You're just faking so you can go home," Melody told her.

"If you won't help me," Liza said bravely, "I'll have to do it myself."

Melody and Howie looked at each other, feeling guilty as Liza headed across the playground. "We should help her," Melody said.

"And Eddie," Howie said.

They both raced toward Mr. Drake, Eddie, Ben, and Liza. But they were too late.

Liza had stopped right in front of Mr. Drake. Melody couldn't believe what Liza was doing.

"Liza," Melody squealed. "What did you do?"

Liza moaned. "I told you I didn't feel well."

Mr. Drake stared at the kids and his eyes flashed red. Then he slowly looked down at his brand-new black cowboy boots. They didn't look brand-new anymore.

Mr. Drake looked paler than usual, but he didn't say a word. He pointed toward the school. Melody, Eddie, and Howie

hustled Liza off to the nurse's office. Ben took off toward the kickball game.

"I can't believe you threw up on Count Dracula's boots," Eddie said with a grin. "That's what I call an original Dracula cure!"

"I guess you weren't faking after all," Melody told her. "Are you feeling better?"

Liza moaned and shook her head. "I'm feeling worse. We're in serious trouble. There's no telling what the most powerful of all vampires will do to us now!"

12

GO JUICE

Two days later, Liza trotted across the playground before school to meet up with her friends. Howie and Eddie cheered for Liza, but Melody was strangely quiet.

"You're a hero!" Eddie said.

"I'm a hero for getting sick on Mr. Drake's boots?" Liza asked.

"No," Howie told her. "You're a hero for getting rid of Count Dracula."

"Me?" Liza asked. "How could I have gotten rid of Mr. Drake? I've been home sick for two days!"

Eddie laughed. "We always knew garlic was a cure for vampires," Eddie said. "What we didn't know is that Count Dracula would fly away if his shoes were messed up by a sick kid. He packed up his duffel bag and left town that afternoon."

For the first time in a week a rosy color returned to Liza's cheeks. "It must have been that spaghetti and garlic bread I had for lunch that day," Liza said. "I wonder if the other teachers will be back to normal now."

"Teachers are never normal," Eddie reminded her.

"Especially when they're all drinking Mr. Drake's bottled vampire juice," Liza added.

Howie shook his head and dug in his backpack to pull out an empty bottle. "I think we may have jumped to conclusions," he admitted. He turned the bottle so his friends could see the label. "I found this in Principal Davis' trash can."

"GO JUICE?" Eddie read after squinting at the label. "I never would've thought to call bottled blood GO JUICE."

Melody carefully read the label. "This isn't blood," she said. "It's an energy drink!"

"Why would teachers need to guzzle an energy drink?" Eddie asked.

Liza stared at Eddie. "Isn't it obvious?" she asked.

"They need extra energy to deal with you," Howie explained.

Eddie pretended to wipe sweat from his forehead. "Whew!" he said. "I guess it's a good thing Mr. Drake flew the coop and took the rest of that GO JUICE with him. The last thing we need around here is a gaggle of supercharged teachers!"

"Mr. Drake did leave one thing behind," Howie told her.

"What?" Liza asked.

"He left his cowboy boots," Eddie said with a huge laugh. Liza and Howie laughed, too.

Not Melody. She leaned against the tree and held her stomach. "I don't feel very well," she said.

"Oh, no," Liza said. "I bet you're catching the same flu bug I had."

"Tell me quick," Eddie said. "What did you have for dinner last night?"

Melody groaned. "Pizza," she said, "with extra garlic."

Eddie's eyes sparkled and he pulled on Melody's arm. "I know just what to do," he said to Melody.

"Are you taking her to the nurse's office?" Howie asked.

Eddie shook his head. "Are you kidding?" he said. "We may have gotten rid of Count Dracula, but we still have another vampire at Bailey School to contend with. I'm taking Melody to see our teacher, and I'm aiming her right for Mrs. Jeepers' feet!"

Debbie Dadey and Marcia Thornton Jones have fun writing stories together. When they both worked at an elementary school in Lexington, Kentucky, Debbie was the school librarian and Marcia was a teacher. During their lunch break in the school cafeteria, they came up with the idea of the Bailey School Kids.

Recently, Debbie and her family moved to Fort Collins, Colorado. Marcia and her husband still live in Kentucky, where she continues to teach. How do these authors write together? They talk on the phone and use computers and fax machines!

Learn more about Debbie and Marcia at their Web site, www.BaileyKids.com!

Think *your* school's scary?

Welcome to Sleepy Hollow Elementary, where everyone says the basement is haunted. But no one's ever gone downstairs to prove it. Until now. Jeff and Cassidy have just found out their classroom has moved to the basement. The creepy haunted basement!
And you thought *your* school was spooky...?

www.scholastic.com/books

GVET